HAPPY END-INGS

A Story About Suffixes

by **Robin Pulver**
illustrated by
Lynn Rowe Reed

Holiday House / New York

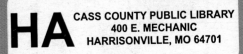

For my cousin, Helen Edinger.
She's a wonder**ful** teach**er**,
and I couldn't be proud**er**!

R. P.

To the clever
and witty
Robin Pulver

L. R. R.

Text copyright © 2011 by Robin Pulver
Illustrations copyright © 2011 by Lynn Rowe Reed
All Rights Reserved
HOLIDAY HOUSE is registered in the U.S. Patent and Trademark Office.
Printed and Bound in October 2010 at Tien Wah Press,
Johor Bahru, Johor, Malaysia.
The text typeface is Agenda Medium.
The artwork was painted in acrylic on canvas and digitally reproduced.
www.holidayhouse.com
First Edition
1 3 5 7 9 10 8 6 4 2

Library of Congress Cataloging-in-Publication Data
Pulver, Robin.
Happy endings : a story about suffixes / by Robin Pulver ; illustrated by Lynn Rowe Reed. — 1st ed.
p. cm.
Summary: When Mr. Wright makes his students study word endings on the last day of school,
even the suffixes rebel.
ISBN 978-0-8234-2296-8 (hardcover)
[1. English language—Suffixes and prefixes—Fiction. 2. Schools—Fiction.]
I. Reed, Lynn Rowe, ill. II. Title.
PZ7.P97325Hap 2011
[Fic]—dc22
2010024066

The school year was winding down. The days seemed endless. Mr. Wright's students were excited about summer vacation.

The word end**ing**s were excited too.

Mr. Wright had written them on the board.

Their turn had come at last.

Finally!

After so much stand**ing** by and watch**ing** and wait**ing**!

Three cheer**s** for word ending**s**!

Also known as suffix**es**.

Mr. Wright announced, "This afternoon we'll be studying word endings, or suffixes. Word endings are your friends. They help with tough words in reading."

At that moment, every ending in the room was a happy ending.

But the kid**s** were in no mood for study**ing**.

Mr. Wright, you must be kidd**ing**!

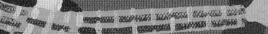

The kids kept fussing.

We're already smarter than we were when school started.

"I know you kids are restless," said Mr. Wright. "Nevertheless, next year you'll be expected to know word endings. But right now, it's time to be lining up for the cafeteria."

The kids forgot everything they learned about school rules and good manners. They butted and budged and pushed.

Mr. Wright sent the rudest and noisiest kids to the end of the line.

"Being at the end is what you get for behaving badly."

As the kids walked away,

Mr. Wright reminded them: "After lunch and our read-aloud, we'll tackle word endings."

Watching and listening, the word endings were stunned.

They're going to tackle us!! Yikes! What does Mr. Wright mean by tackling us? Why would they do that? We're not the enemy! And we're not playing football!

Are we being punished? Is that why we're at the ends of the words?

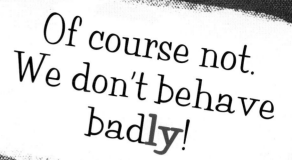

Of course not.
We don't behave
bad**ly**!

Now every end**ing**
was a sad end**ing**.

We don't do anything wrong!

The word endings slipped off the board. They headed for the gym to work out.

This situation is getting hairy. We're splitting!

NO RUNNING IN HALL

GYM →

Meanwhile, in the cafeteria, the kids were acting up.
They were throwing food, yelling, and goofing off.

After lunch their exasperated
teacher announced: "We're skipping
read-aloud. We're going right into
studying word endings."
The kids protested.

But it's the last chapter
of *Ace Scooper,
Dog Detective*!

"You'll have to make up your own end**ing**," said Mr. Wright. "It's time to tackle suffix**es**."

He point**ed** at the board. Then he star**ed**. "Good grief," he said. "This is the crazi**est** year of my teach**ing** life! No summer vacation until the word end**ings** are found. Seriously!"

Vacationless!

"We're doomed!" groaned the kids. Suddenly, word endings were terribly important. The kids wanted them back.

The kids got busy making and putting up posters.

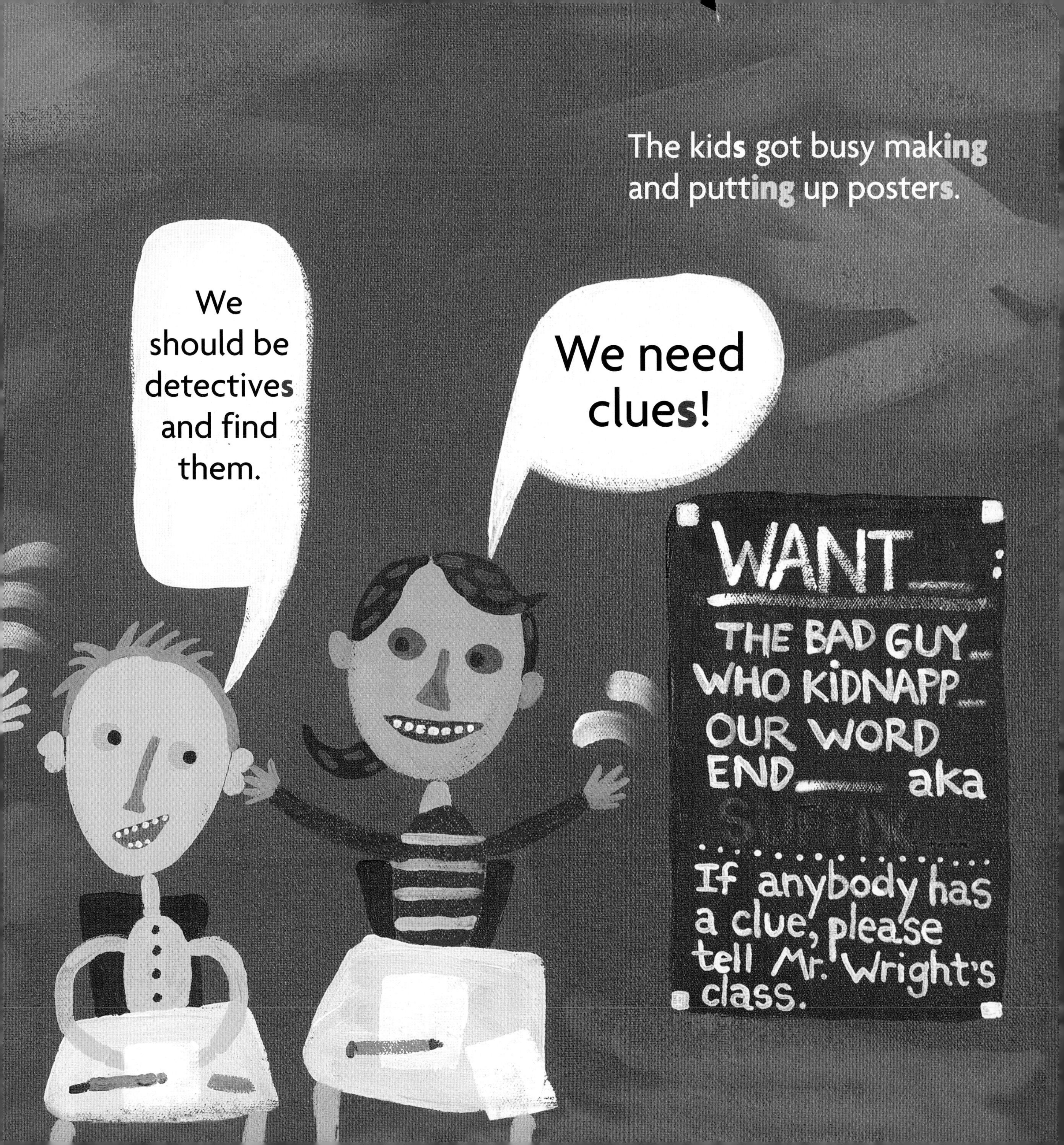

Meanwhile, in the gym, the suffix**es** were do**ing** push-up**s** and pull-up**s**. They were runn**ing** and jump**ing**, bounc**ing** and balanc**ing**.

Finally, they felt strong**er**. They felt brav**er** too. They start**ed** back to the classroom. In the hall they spott**ed** the poster**s**.

Hey! The kid**s** are look**ing** for us!

The word end**ings** decid**ed** to
hide and make up clue**s**. This
was their big chance to go first.

Try ing clean
out your
s desk!
Hurry! We're
ing suffocat!

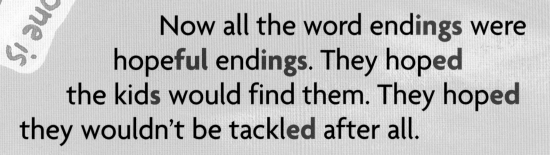

Now all the word end**ings** were
hope**ful** end**ings**. They hop**ed**
the kid**s** would find them. They hop**ed**
they wouldn't be tackl**ed** after all.

The kids found the clues in plain sight.
At first they were impossible to read.
But finally:

Aha!
We figur**ed**
it out!

The end**ings**
come first in
these mix**ed**-up
words!

If we move
them to the
end where
they belong,
we can read
the clue**s**.

ing to the end of clean

s to the end of desk

ing to the end of suffocat

ing to the end of get

ed to the end of pok

ing to the end of miss

s to the end of scissor

ing to the end of hid

est to the end of messi

y to the end of Yuck

ed to the end of chew

y to the end of Dirt

er to the end of gross

y to the end of Mold

s to the end of crumb

ful to the end of mouth

y to the end of Luck

s to the end of win

ness to the end of neat

less to the end of spot

"Thanks to these clues," the kids exclaimed,
"we don't have to search endlessly!"
They talked Mr. Wright into letting them
clean out their desks.

MILK

Thank good**ness**
we found you!

Thank good**ness** this
day is near**ly** over!

Mr. Wright smiled and opened *Ace Scooper, Dog Detective* to the last chapter. When he started to read, the kids settled down and listened.

Thank goodness the puppy is safe!

He's free at last!

And so are we!

When Mr. Wright announced "The End," everyone rejoiced.

Finally, summer vacation stretched ahead, promising days of endless fun.

END OF YEAR REPORT CARDS

CLASS ASSIGNMENTS FOR NEXT YEAR

Mrs. Edinger

Every ending leads to a new beginning!

Look! She is us!

The end

Word endings, or suffixes, are letter groups that are added to the end of a base word or root.

root + **ing** = root**ing**

I'm root**ing** for you as you tackle suffix**es**!

We'll be help**ful**!

I'm a suffix too!

If a word looks too hard, you can sometimes figure it out by looking at the ending first, e.g., winding, endless, teacher. Sometimes words that look long and hard have two or three endings in a row:

endlessness (two suffixes)
playfully (two suffixes)
truthfully (two suffixes)
surprisingly (two suffixes)
frighteningly (three suffixes!)

Here are some help**ful** rule**s** about add**ing** suffix**es** to word**s**:

 1 If the base word has a long vowel before the final consonant, drop the e to add **-ing** or **-ed**:

    hope + **-ing** or **-ed** = hop**ing** or hop**ed** (Drop the e! It won't break!)

    tape + **-ing** or **-ed** = tap**ing** or tap**ed**

2 If the base word has a short vowel before the final consonant, DOUBLE the consonant before add**ing** the suffix:

    drop + **-ed** or **-ing** = dropp**ed** or dropp**ing**

    hop + **-ed** or **-ing** = hopp**ed** or hopp**ing**

    tap + **-ed** or **-ing** = tapp**ed** or tapp**ing**

Exceptions!: live + **-ing** = liv**ing**

    come + **-ing** = com**ing**

3 When adding **-ly** or **-est** to a base word ending in y, change the y to i:

    happy + **-ly** = happi**ly**

    happy + **-est** = happi**est**

4 To make a plural of a base word that ends in a consonant followed by a y, change the y to i and add **-es**.

    More than one reply = repl**ies**

    More than one supply = suppl**ies**

    (What is more than one lady?)

There are many more suffixes. Some other suffixes, such as **ant**, **ent**, **ive**, **ion**, and **y**, are even in this book. Finding out about suffixes helps you learn new words!

Don't worry! You'll get it!

You must be power**fully** proud of yourself for read**ing** those long word**s**!

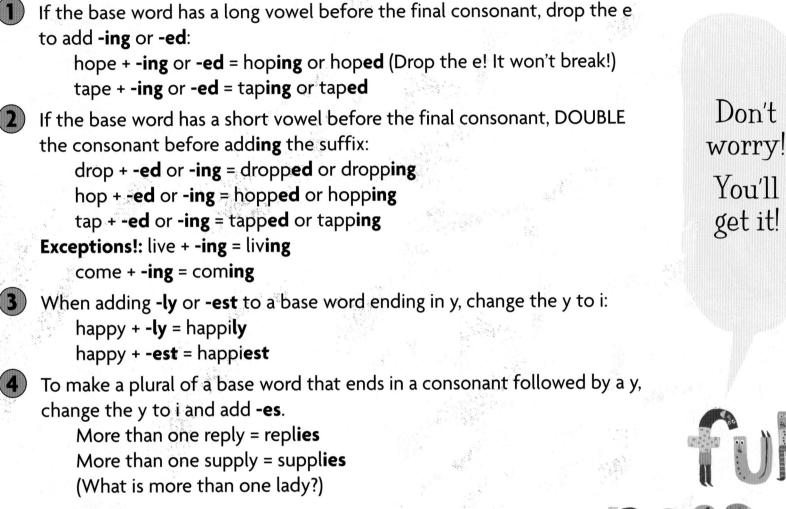

Here are some clue**s** to help with word end**ings**, aka suffix**es**:

Add me to a verb and you've got the person who's doing the action.
> teach + **-er** = teach**er** (the person who teach**es**)
> (What do you call a person who paint**s**?)

We're add**ed** to noun**s** to make them plural.
> One bunch, two bunch**es**
> (What is more than one book?)

Usually I hook onto an adjective. I like to be fast**est** and smart**est**.
But when I'm lazi**est**, I'm also the slow**est**.
> (What chang**ed** in lazy?)

Add**ed** to the end of a noun, I make an adjective.
> chill**y**, sleep**y**, rain**y**
> (How do you make an adjective out of **grouch**?)

Add me to an adjective to make a noun!
> kind**ness**, gross**ness**, mean**ness**
> (Can you make a noun out of **dark**?)

Add**ed** to the end of a noun, I make it go away.
> **Fearless**! **Spotless**!
> (Make hair go away: **Hair____** !)

If you add me to week (week**ly**), it means every week. If you do something month**ly**,
how often is that? What about year**ly**? What does dai**ly** mean? (Hint: a y changed to an i.)
> I can also make an adjective out of a noun. If you have many friend**s**,
> you must be a **friend____** person!

I can make a word be full of itself.
> joy**ful** means full of joy
> fear**ful** means full of fear
> (What does hope**ful** mean?)

Add me to a verb to make it past tense.
> Walk**ed** is the past tense of walk.

> Look for other helpful suffixes, such as **-ous**, **-ion**, **-en**, **-ive**. They'll help with tack**ling** tough words too!